ROCKET BOY

SPACEFLIGHT BOOK

DOUGLAS ROTHMAN

AND

ARIANA ROSENBERG

AuthorHouse™
1663 Liberty Drive
Bloomington, IN 47403
www.authorhouse.com
Phone: 833-262-8899

Because of the dynamic nature of the Internet, any web addresses or links contained in this book may have changed
since publication and may no longer be valid. The views expressed in this work are solely those of the author and do not
necessarily reflect the views of the publisher, and the publisher hereby disclaims any responsibility for them.

Any people depicted in stock imagery provided by Getty Images are models,
and such images are being used for illustrative purposes only.
Certain stock imagery © Getty Images.

This book is printed on acid-free paper.

ISBN: 978-1-6655-5939-3 (sc)
ISBN: 978-1-6655-5938-6 (e)

Print information available on the last page.

Published by AuthorHouse 05/09/2022

authorHOUSE®

Author

Douglas Rothman
Scottsdale, Arizona

Editor and Co-Author

Ariana Rosenberg
Perth, WA Australia

CONTENTS

PROLOGUE / OUTLINE: ROCKET

This children's book takes place in Boise, Idaho, where a fourteen-year-old boy named Talon seems to be a very average boy at first but has a large imagination. He tries to win his school science fair by rebuilding a used space rocket ship that USAF Capt. Tom Hanson flew into space years earlier.

A local scrap yard, named Apollo's Scrapyard, provides the resources for Talon's science project. Bart, the owner of Apollo's Scrapyard, is eager to help Talon, assuming he has real intentions to launch it into space.

Talon's project is put on hold after a close call that put Talon's life in real physical danger. The rocket capsule had a ballistic charge built into the emergency exit hatch, and it discharges. This close call shuts down Talon's project and even makes the evening local news. The story is picked up as a human interest story, syndicated to other stations, and is broadcast into the home of Tom Hanson, the captain who retired as a two-star general.

This general sees the old rocket, the same one he flew into space seventeen years earlier, on the news. This brings back precious memories for General Hanson, and he is now determined to find the location and pay his rocket, and Talon, a visit.

The general holds a key to Talon's project that re-motivates Talon to finish what he had started.

The general also has a unique gift for Talon: his old space helmet and space suit, which no longer fit the General and have remained in his closet for seventeen years.

The rocket is still doomed, though, and is scheduled to be taken down by safety officials in Boise, Idaho. The rocket has five days left before it goes back to the scrapyard for destruction because of safety reasons.

It is now or never for Talon to take his rocket flight. Early the next morning, Talon leaves his mother a note and rides his bike to the launch pad where the rocket sits.

Talon's late grandfather's farm is two short miles Talon's home, and the farm is where Talon will soon make history.

Talon has set everything in motion and the countdown is now ready. For-real? 10–9–8–7–6–5–4–3–2–1–liftoff. Yes, for real!

The city is woken up by a great sound blast from the old Titan II rocket. The rocket rips itself from the launch pad once again.

Talon now begins his trip into space. There is nothing that can stop the rocket once it is set in motion.

This small city is now front page news around the world, as is Talon.

General Tom Hanson wakes up to his morning news to see his young friend and his rocket heading for orbit once again.

The general knows this is no joke, and requires the utmost serious action. He leaps into action and helps Talon fly this rocket from the local air force base.

He guides Talon by UHF radio, and knows Talon knows how to use everything in the capsule. After all, the general taught him only days earlier.

With help from many agencies, Talon is now on way back home to Little Falls Air Force Base, Idaho. Talon's family and many agencies await his arrival. The world awaits his return.

Talon lands safely and is now awarded the top science fair project prize for the entire United States.

The story ends with lessons in life and making dream comes true. The rocket itself ends up as a static museum piece in Little Falls Air Force Base.

The very last chapter has a small twist to the final plot.

The United States president sends off a "Flash One" memo to all military bases: "Do not to send any rockets to any more junkyards for salvage." Bart's scrapyard is having a fantastic year now, selling everything from t-shirts to toy rockets.

Somewhere in this vast scrapyard, a plain, white truck drives up to unload a very large wooden crate.

The crate is marked *Property of United Science Company*. Also on the side of the same crate are the words *Quantum Physics Laboratory*.

As the driver starts to drive away, a small booklet falls out of the box's inventory list and lands on the ground below. The small booklet reads: "Failed science project—time travel." The booklet was plain white in color.

CHAPTER

BOISE, IDAHO, ON ANY TYPICAL DAY

It was an early spring day, and there was not a cloud in the sky. The leaves on the big oak trees had just started turning a bright mint green. My walk to school was not far, no more than six blocks. But my father would always drive me to school in the mornings, and I walked home each day. It allowed me to think about planes and flying.

My walk home was a straight shot down the long street to my house. Both sides of the street were lined with juniper trees that always smelled, to me, like warm cinnamon toast.

I would pull the bark off the branches and smell it all the way home. I could count on being the first one back after school, and always before Robert, my brother. He would eat both snacks that our mom had left out on the kitchen counter for us.

My dad was the best. He helped me build my school projects out in our garage. I liked to hear his stories about putting out fires when he was a firefighter for the forest service. Now, he works for the parks service dealing with fishing licenses.

We both like to watch science shows on television, and we had spent a lot of time talking about the future—my future, and what I would like to do when I grew up. I really wanted to be an astronaut, like the ones on the space shuttles.

I thought about what it would take to be an astronaut, and how I could become one as soon as possible.

I would spend hours daydreaming about my future adventures and what it would be like in my own spaceship, commanding a mission to the moon or maybe even to Mars.

My two closest friends were in the same grade as me; Tony and Steven.

Tony had just moved to Idaho that year with his mom, dad, and little brother. Even though he had just moved, I thought we were best friends. I had known Steven for six years. I don't remember where he used to live, but he traveled a lot during the summers with his parents. We never got many chances to hang out or play videogames.

CHAPTER

THE IDEA

There were about four weeks left until school was out for the summer. All my friends were starting to plan their summer vacations already, or hoping that summer would come sooner rather than later.

One day after school, Tony came up to me, holding a magazine article. It was about a man in Florida who had built a huge rocket that could send him into orbit around the earth, although it was never finished. The man could not obtain a real space suit or helmet. Plus the city didn't allow it.

Tony and I were thinking how easy it looked to possibly build a rocket out of junkyard parts for our school science fair. What if our rocket worked and could send all three of us into space? We talked about it all day and late into the evening, until each of us had to go home for dinner. Tony and Steven soon forgot about the rocket, shortly after playing video games that night.

I looked at the article again before going to bed. It said, "The ex-fireman, who was now retired in Florida, was building the rocket for an extreme hobby." It went on to say, "Thomas Tyrell had no intentions of actually launching his rocket currently or in the future. It was just to see if he could make it."

I read the article about twenty times. I wrote down everything I could that would help us build our rocket and get the parts we would need.

Tony and I even knew where we could get some rocket parts. We would get them from the local scrapyard just a few blocks away from my grandfather's farm.

I paused for a minute as I thought about my late grandfather, who passed away just after Thanksgiving last year. I started to fall asleep, still holding onto the magazine article in my right hand. I looked at a picture of my grandfather on the wall; the photo was in black and white. He was standing in front of his new truck—a Ford 150, I think they called it.

I miss him, I thought to myself, closing my eyes and dreaming of many things.

The next day after school, Tony and Steven came over to my house before my parents went off to work. We all went to Apollo's Scrapyard, which was about three miles away. It was near the large Pine Top grocery store that everyone knew of and shopped at.

It took us about ten minutes to ride to Apollo's on our bikes. The place was huge and had old car parts at one end and old planes at the other.

The military sold the old planes years ago for scrap metal. We crawled under the wire fence at the back of the junkyard. There was a hole in it that we used sometimes to hang out on the weekend and throw rocks at the old parts.

As we were walking towards the front of the junkyard, Tony said he thought he saw the workers a few days ago bring in something that looked like a rocket from McNeil Air Force Base.

I remembered my dad saying that air force base had closed a few years ago. Before we knew it, we were standing in front of what looked like a small rocket—a spaceship.

It was about fifteen feet tall and had enough room for two, maybe three, people to fit in. Steven said it looked like they took everything out of it, even though he didn't know what it was. It was fun to pretend like we knew what we were doing and think about if it had ever flown before. We all wondered: where did it come from? Did it really go into space? Had there been real astronauts in it? It was perfect. It was perfect for our project.

We looked at each other, and at the exact same time, we all said, "Let's build a rocket like that guy in Florida. Yah, let's do it."

It was going to be awesome; no one would believe that we were going to build a spaceship rocket.

I said, "How are we going to get it out of here? And will Bart let us have it?"

Steven said, "I will talk to my brother. You know he buys a lot of parts from Bart for his car. Bart and he are pretty good friends. My parents know him as well."

Everyone in town knew Apollo's Scrapyard, gas station, TV repair shop, and candy store. They all had free storytelling at this location. This place was one of the first buildings in my quiet, little city. Bart's father had owned it before him, and his father before him. It was a labyrinth of many things to see. Who knew where it all came from?

This rocket could work. After all, it looked like it was built for space and did go there before, I thought to myself.

I said, "If we all work together, we can do this, and it will be perfect for our school science project."

The end of the day came too soon as we said goodbye to each other. We climbed back under the fence to our bikes, and back home we went.

As we each set course for home on our bikes, we each envisioned how the rocket would look in the days and weeks to come. We knew it would be very difficult to complete such a project. But we were determined and ready for the challenge ahead of us.

It was not long, only two days, before we returned to the scrapyard. This time, we went to the office where Bart was sitting, reading the local newspaper.

"Morning boys!" Bart said to us. "So you think you're going to build yourselves a space rocket?"

We all looked bewildered about how Bart knew about our plans.

"Sure, we're not only going to build it; we are going to fly it into space. But how did you know that, sir?" I answered his question with a half-smile on my face.

"Well, son, news travels fast in this town. And besides, Andy told me yesterday when he came in for a rear light for his car," Bart said.

Andy was Steven's older brother.

Bart chuckled and said, "Let me know when you are going to launch that thing. I want to take a picture of that." He then moved his newspaper across his face.

We were too young to notice the subtle brush-off.

"How much for the rocket?" I asked Bart.

"Well, that depends how much you have, young man," Bart said over his newspaper.

I said, "1,750 dollars."

The newspaper slowly came down, exposing Bart's eyes. "You must mean $17.50."

"No, sir. My grandfather left me some money when he passed away last year. My mom put it in a bank account at Main Street Bank."

"You don't say," Bart said as he looked up and to the right. "Your parents would never let you buy such a thing. And besides, where would you put it? In your backyard?"

"That is a good question," I said to Bart. I seemed to be in charge of the conversation, and his attention. "We have been thinking of buying this rocket and would like to use it for a school science project. All of us are going to try to rebuild it and win. We want to move it to my grandfather's farmhouse that has a large concrete pad. It has large chains that will hold the rocket down in case any wind or storm should try to knock it down."

I unfolded a large piece of white paper from the right rear pocket of my jeans. It had the plans all drawn out in detail.

Bart looked over Talon's plans as if he was going to fly the rocket himself. He said nothing for a few minutes, and just made sounds like, "Hum, oh-yah"

As he rubbed his chin with his right hand, Bart said, "I see. Yes this just could work."

Bart looked up as he came around from behind the counter, putting on his worn leather gloves at the same time. Bart paused for a minute and said, "I tell you what, Talon. I am going to help you boys out and I am going to just give this rocket to you for free. Heck, no one would want to buy a rocket around here anyway. And it would be a complete shame not to see it put to some good for science or a summer project. I will just need your parents to come by the shop and give me $50.00 to move it to your Grandfather's farm." Bart paused. "I am sorry to hear he passed away; too bad. I remember he purchased a Ferguson T035 water pump from me three years ago—or was it the TE-20? I forget. Yes, too bad Talon, very nice man. Well, you do him proud now and complete this space rocket."

"Orbiter capsule is the correct name, sir," Talon said with confidence and pride.

"Yah, sure, Talon. Star orbiter capsule ship," Bart repeated a few times under his breath. After walking outside to look at it up close, Bart ended the conversation by saying, "Just make sure your parents bring by the $50.00. I will need that to move it." As Bart walked back into his store, he said again to himself, "Star orbiter capsule."

CHAPTER

THE CHECKLIST

Now that the largest part of the boys' project was completed by securing the orbiter capsule and second-stage rocket, the boys directed their attention to the things that go inside a rocket.

Five days later, Talon persuaded his parents the rocket would be part of a large science project for school. It was delivered to his grandfather's farm that afternoon. Bart was there for the delivery as well.

"I told your son," Bart said to Talon's father.

"I remember when I built myself a ham radio when I was his age, but I guess things just get bigger and better as time goes on."

Talon's father did not say much; he just made sure the $50.00 was counted out, with a tip to the driver for his extra help. Talon's father was like any other father, if that father preferred reading books over watching TV, and working out in the yard just about any chance he could. Kind and considerate, he never yelled or showed his temper, if he had any. If anything that stuck out, it would have to be that Talon's father always loved to end any conversation with the phrase, "All right'ie then." *I'm lucky to have such good parents*, he thought as his father counted out the money into Bart's hand.

As Bart left, driving back down the dirt road heading north, back to town, the dust kicked up behind the big flatbed truck. It took about a good five minutes to disappear from their sight.

"All right'ie then," Talon's father said to him, "let's see what we have here. I have to say, Talon, I am a bit excited to see this myself." *Well sometimes at the beginning of a sentence too*, Talon thought, considering his father's habit.

"Dad, look at this. It has a radio already in it. And wow, oh yeah, look here…not there. Wow, oh man. Look at this Dad." Talon was so excited his eyes could not focus on any one thing, nor could his thoughts catch up with his sight.

"UHF-VHF radio they call this Talon. I have some experience with this from my days in the military before you were born."

"Could you show me how to use it dad?" Talon asked his father.

"Yes, all right'ie then, first you must turn the battery on here…I see, it might need some charging. And then we can—stop, wait one minute. Would you look at this?" Something wedged in the lower right side of the lower console panel had caught his father's eye. He reached down inside the capsule and, with his right hand and fingers extended as far as they would reach, he slowly wedged a small piece of plastic between his right index finger and his second finger, as if he was crossing his two fingers in making a promise.

"Yes, yes, I have it…no, darn…wait one minute…okay, I think we have it now. Come to papa. Okay…wait, wait! Darn," Talon's father said. "All right'ie then, Talon, it's your turn. I cannot reach it. Do you see it Talon? Right there next to that thing, that looks like that thing, you know."

Talon reached down into the dust and trash that had blown into the inner capsule over time, over the years as it sat there looking up into the open sky. Talon's hands reached down and plucked it up from the hidden area. It was hard to see just looking into the capsule from the outside. "I got it," he said, his hands now firmly grasping a plastic two-ring binder sort of thing. "What is it dad?"

"Talon, do you know what this is?" his dad said while looking it over in his hands.

"What, dad?" Talon replied, looking at the many pieces of single paper encased in individual pieces of plastic.

"It's a checklist from the last real astronaut who must have flown this rocket into space."

"Orbit, dad. The orbiter goes into orbit not space," Talon said to his dad, using his knowledge from his studies on science and space.

"Look, Talon, his name and initials are still on this. *Lieutenant Captain Tom Hanson.* He was that guy that went around the earth for five days in this. You were about five years old then, Talon."

Talon's father was very surprised by this large piece of real history in his hands.

The rocket now stood proud on his grandfather's farm. Both Talon and his father just stood there and, backing up a little, looked up, up, at this great rocket. Talon's father took his ball cap off his head and held it in his right hand to his right hip, in a show of respect for the courage that it took to fly this up into orbit, 250 miles up into space.

As the pair thought about the history of the rocket, they also looked around Talon's grandfather's farm. As his grandfather grew older, he required extra oxygen. So when they found a couple of these canisters in the shed, neither was surprised. Talon grinned, thinking, *This is brilliant! If the rocket does go to space, there will be oxygen.* Talon's father took him back outside after they looked around for a few more minutes.

Talon's father said to his son, "It must have been hard for Captain Tom Hanson up there. He was all alone, maybe afraid or not, and he spent five long days and nights in space. If an emergency occurred, there was nothing and no one who could help him. He truly was a hero and real adventurist and astronaut."

They both just stood there looking up. No more words were spoken. Father and son, shoulder to almost shoulder.

CHAPTER

THE CAPSULE

The next morning was Saturday. Talon did not waste any time eating breakfast and cleaning his room before heading over to his grandfather's farm to meet Tony and Steven and start working on the rocket.

His father dropped him off on the way to town. "I will pick you back up around four p.m. Talon. Okay? Four p.m.," his father said to him as he slowly drove away, taking one more look at the dusty white and blue rocket.

Talon's father had loaned Talon many of his hand tools to tinker with the many things to tinker with in and on the capsule.

For young men, Talon, Tony, and Steven had a well laid-out plan to clean up this piece of history and restore it to peak condition.

Almost everything was taken out of the tall rocket the very first day, and laid out in a nice, neat line.

"We need to divide up the necessary parts and equipment to build it to fly in six weeks. Is that the launch time we have agreed on guys?"

Tony said, "Sure, that sounds good to me, although I will have to be back that week for my mom's birthday. Each year my dad forgets it, and this year she is asking him to take her to that new restaurant that opened this year."

Steven said, "Oh yes, we went there last week. The Burger Cave. They have great fries. I think it might be bring your own food, like a picnic place."

Steven set down a large piece of pipe he had just taken out of the cockpit of the rocket. The pipe had a yellow and red sticker on it which read 02. "Hey Talon, what do you make of this *02?*"

"I am not sure," said Talon, "just label it and I will ask Mr. Perkins all of our questions when I am in his science class next week. I have him for second period. Do you have him this year?"

"For now, just set it next to the first pipe we took out. Maybe they have it all numbered like watercolor painting."

"Okay," Steven said. "I will look for the 03 pipe then."

"Me too," said Tony.

"I forgot the summer is almost over, and it's a good thing because we are going to need some help from some schoolteachers."

"My dad is good with electronics and metals," said Tony. "I am not sure about rocket fuel though."

"Rocket fuel," they all said at the exact same time. "How are we going to find rocket fuel? Isn't that stuff dangerous?"

Talon remembered some time ago that Bart had told him an alternative rocket fuel. Something about kerosene and alcohol. Something that might already be on the farm.

"I am not sure that my dad would allow me to keep it in our garage," Tony said to everyone.

Before the boys knew it, the sun was dipping behind the traditional red cedar barn.

Talon knew he had about thirty minutes left before his dad would be there to pick him up. So Talon said, "Guys, my dad will be here in fifteen minutes. Can we all meet tomorrow again?"

And for the very first time, Talon could see a tiny bit of interest in the project from Tony and Steven.

"Well, okay, I guess I can make it tomorrow. I have not played my new video game my parents gave me last week: *Twisters and Nuron Gorg* yet," said Tony.

"Nice," said Steven. "You have that? It just came out two weeks ago. Can I come over and play it with you tomorrow?"

"Okay. I will see you later, Talon," said Tony and Steven as they rode their bicycles off the road, taking the short cut through two farms, one cattle ranch, and fourteen streets to their homes.

Talon looked at the many items taken from this capsule, and it sounded hollow now from not having the items in it. Tomorrow he would vacuum and wash the inside.

The very last item Talon looked at before his father started making his way up the long driveway leading to the concrete pad was a small, black box, and on this black box was a label: *Ballistic Charge Caution.* Talon did not think much of it and set it down in the long line of things, gadgets, and gauges.

Until tomorrow! he thought.

ASSEMBLE ROCKET

Before Talon knew it, almost a week had gone by. He had cleaned and washed the inside and outside of the entire rocket ship. He even put a coat of car polish on the whole outside of the rocket.

He had been studying every small detail of traveling into space, using the internet, and also many adult opinions and ideas from teachers and friends of his parents.

Talon studied the checklist that was left behind, remembering every detail.

It was the third week of school, and many of Talon's science teachers had already been tremendously helpful to him, explaining math, science, and electronics, and what they all meant to him and the craft. They were all excited about him bringing it to the science fair in the spring.

The space craft was seen as a great achievement by all his fellow students. They were all quite amazed that Talon had taken it this far, with little to no help from his friends, who had used their time for other important things, like achieving the number one spot on *Twisters and Gorges*. Even Talon's father seemed to have lost interest in driving Talon to his grandfather's farm. The farm also might be up for sale soon, as no one seemed to be interested in farming anymore.

Talon's brother made jokes about how they should turn the rocket into a forty-foot-tall chicken coop.

The only one who seemed to want to see the project through to the end was Bart from Apollo's Junkyard, who was working with Talon to get the UHF radio to work with his ham radio. A couple of Talon's teachers had also taken a real interest in his project.

"Spring break will be here in three weeks, dear," Talon's mother said to her husband specifically, but the words were not unnoticed by all. She was cutting and placing slices of pecan pie in front of each of her family members, almost as if to prepare them for bad news. Pecan pie was Talon's favorite.

"You don't say, dear," her husband replied automatically, without looking up from his newspaper.

"Yes, it is time for us all to go to my sister's place in California for the week."

"Wow, how time flies," he replied. "We had such a good time last year, I thought we could skip a year or two, or three."

"Very funny, dear. No, it is that time again. I know we have a lot on our plates, but I really want to see my sister before she adopts another stray dog or two."

"Yes, I am still cleaning out the Milk Bones from my sleeping bag," her husband said, folding his newspaper and preparing for defeat.

The sweet smell of the warm pecan pie was now in full effect. She felt it was time to finish her checklist of things to do before spring break and during.

She said to her husband, "Dear, here's your checklist for the trip. I hope you don't mind, but I have made it out for you all ready."

"Okay, are you men ready? One, get the sleeping bags cleaned and ready for trip. Two, have the oil in the car replaced. Three, plant the flower bulbs in the front garden before we go. Four, take the rocket back to the junkyard, in preparation for the land to be sold off. Five, fix the broken window in the back door."

"Wait, wait!" Talon said. "Remove the rocket? How? Why? I mean, why? Can't we just wait until winter and—"

She knew Talon would be very upset about that one, even disappointed.

"Well, we can't keep it forever, Talon. I mean, were you expecting to fly it into space for real? You and your father had gone into this with the idea it was going to be for a major school project, right? And isn't that coming up in two weeks? That will give us a week to donate it to a park or something. But it makes the farm impossible to sell, with a huge rocket standing in the backyard."

Talon's brother chimed in with a snide comment. "Mom, can't we just make it into that chicken coop?"

His mom said, "That was not nice. Can't you see your brother is upset about this, and jokes are not the answer we need right now?"

"You have two weeks left, Talon—two weeks to figure it out before we all go on vacation, isn't that right dear?" She looked for confirmation from her husband.

"Uh-huh," he said, nodding to his wife.

"No pie for me, Mom," said Talon, as he slowly slid his plate away from his sight to the middle of the table. "I am going to go to ride my bike over to grandpa's farm and work on it a little bit tonight."

"Sure, you go ahead sweetheart. Just be careful and take my cell phone with you. I will call you, or your father will, when we are coming to pick you up." She grabbed the cell phone from her left apron pocket and handed it to him.

Without any goodbyes, Talon picked up his coat, got on his bike, and began the three-mile ride down the road, behind the big cedar trees, and behind the long rows of baled straw. He went down the road to work on the rocket he would soon have to forget about. At this point, all the equipment had been reinstalled and tested by Bart and Talon's father. All of the equipment checked out. It was ready to go.

It did not take him long to reach the location where he had spent the last five weeks working on this huge undertaking.

Even from the road, passersby could see the huge white rocket standing tall, as if it was getting ready for a second chance to take one astronaut into orbit.

Almost all the components had been cleaned and reinstalled. All of them had been tested with Bart's help to make sure they work and fix the ones that did not. But he knew there was always the issue of real rocket fuel, and, of course, the very real possibility of getting injured or worse if he did try to take off in this rocket. He remembered the words of his dad that no one on this earth could have helped Captain Tom Hanson if something had gone wrong when he went into orbit. He was a real trained astronaut, and even had his own car.

Talon went to pick up one of the last items: an orange box. All he could remember was that he had picked it up—that one item that was labeled *Ballistic Charge—Caution*. He had grabbed and pulled a wire cord attached to a high explosive device used to open the door hatch in the event of an emergency in the water. It was carelessly never removed before the rocket was sent to the salvage yard and again resold to Bart's junkyard.

Boom! Without a second's warning, the device let out such a load explosive sound, it rocked the homes in a one-mile area, and the sound wave carried for miles in the still of the night, beyond the long rows of straw bales, beyond the rows of large cedars, three miles down, and into the kitchen of Talon's house, where his mom was cleaning the last plate of pecan pie.

The kitchen windows rattled some, and she knew it was a sound no mother would ever want to hear. Talon's father had heard it as well, as did Robert, who wished he had not said anything about a chicken coop. Without words, they all went outside and stood next to their Ford pickup truck, Talon's mom with her apron still on.

Talon's dad said very calmly and distinctly, "Dear, why don't you call Talon on your cell phone and tell him we are coming to pick him up?"

Her hands went right for her left apron pocket, where she always kept her cell phone, knowing if her right hand was wet, she could always grab it with her dry left hand—as she had done when she handed it to Talon to take with him.

"Here, use mine dear," as her husband drove and attempted to keep calm, saying nothing about the hellish cannon shot sound that came from the direction of the farm. She tried to dial his phone but could not unlock the keypad.

"All right'ie then," he said, taking the phone back and dialing.

Talon was stunned and in serious trouble. A small, amber fire had taken control of some of the grass due to the heat of the blast.

His parents and brother were 500 feet away from the driveway when they clearly saw smoke and a small fire right next to the rocket.

The Ford came to a complete stop when they saw Talon start to get up and walk off on his own. He had singe marks around his jacket and pants legs where the ballistic charge had discharged when he pulled the bright orange cord attached to the small but powerful charge.

Talon's parents were obviously upset at the entire incident, but very happy he was not injured at all. The local farmers called the local fire department, and before anyone knew it, it was a major event on the local news.

It was half past midnight before Talon was in his bed, knowing this was the end of his rocket. His parents would never let him go near it let alone try to fly it. Talon was so sad. He just went to bed and did not look up at the stars through his window. He just rolled over and closed his eyes.

CHAPTER

About the same time Talon was closing his eyes in his bed in Boise, Idaho, there was an older man, about fifty-two, who was just getting up for the second time that night, after trying to fall asleep. He was complaining to himself about the noise that was being produced by all the aircraft jet engines on Nickels Air Force Base in southern California.

This middle-aged man had poured himself a full glass of apple juice and sat down to watch a little news about the weather for Thursday. He was going to visit his daughter in Lance, Idaho, about a thirty-minute drive from Boise, Idaho.

Having trouble finding the remote control for the TV always made him feel like he was losing his memory. Most men know that was a part of life and getting older, and the best thing to do was to purchase two remotes and use one when the other had been taken by the remote control gremlin.

Until then, he went on, spilling some of his apple juice on the floor his sleeping wife just cleaned hours earlier. As he cleaned the floor with his left sock, he fumbled for the remote before the news was off for the night.

He checked one last place: under his newspaper on his chair. In doing so, he disturbed what was lying on the arm of the olive drab green chair, upsetting the perfect balance his uniform jacket was relying on to rest. The jacket fell to the floor just in front of the chair.

He was in luck: there was the remote control. He clicked it a few times and was now looking at the news for current and world events.

He returned to the chair to sit down, stepping over his standard issue Air Force NASA-issued jacket, which clearly displayed his name in the upper left corner: *General Tom G. Hanson*.

"Today in Boise, Idaho," the news reporter began, "a young boy tempted fate and all reason when he attempted to rebuild a NASA two-stage Titan manned rocket that was used years ago by then Captain Tom G. Hanson, who made a historic flight into outer space."

"Orbit, lady, orbit—not outer space!" he said in annoyance. As Tom G. Hanson finished his glass of apple juice, he was fully interested in what was unfolding on the news.

The reporter continued. "This boy was not injured while a ballistic charge went off when he was handling it during his school project."

The local news there had taken many pictures of the rocket, and Talon had General Tom G. Hanson's full attention.

The general finished the news, said, "Come on, Buzz," to his faithful tan beagle, and went back to bed for the night. Buzz did stay up for another hour, finding more apple juice to lick up from the floor.

The next day back in Boise, Idaho, it was easy for Talon to wake up and start his day, trying to not talk about what had happened the night before. His parents' home phone was ringing. A few city officials were asking questions about how he got his hands on a rocket in the first place.

He could hear his mom just listening some, then saying, "Yes…no…that's right. Yes. I agree. The rocket must be moved back to the junkyard soon as possible and destroyed."

Talon took down all of the aerial photographs on his walls. They were to help him figure out where he would be in relation to Boise, Idaho if he had ever had a real chance to go in a rocket. He took down the charts on stars to navigate by and radio frequencies he would need to use if he had to cross into other countries in a rocket once in orbit.

He had it all planned out, every step and every necessity one would need in space. Much of it was in manuals that had been inside compartments in the rocket no one had ever taken the time to investigate.

There was even a space bar with raisins and nuts—food that had now grown hard and inedible, but Talon kept it as a keepsake.

His mom came into his room and said, "I am sorry about your accident, and I feel bad that you will not be able to display your rocket for your science fair project in ten days. The city has paid for the removal of it in ten days, and then it will be taken back to the scrapyard. Do you want to go out there tomorrow to get your items and personal things?"

I will be okay with that, Talon thought, saying nothing but nodding his head in agreement.

The excitement for the event in the small town died out rather quickly. The next day turned into three days, and on the fourth day, Talon said he was ready to go get his things, his father's tools, and books, maps, and such.

They got into the Ford truck once again, and the three-mile drive seemed like thirty. At one point, his mom was so distracted by Talon's lack of words, she glanced over at him and smiled, trying to get a response back.

Talon did say, in a snappish loud voice, "Look out mom," as a car horn broke the silence. A small rental was crossing the intersection on the driver's green light while Talon's mom had taken her eyes off the road.

Although there was no contact between vehicles or any smell of rubber, there was a rather stern look from a middle-aged man on his cell phone. He was talking to Susan Ann Ledbetter, a reporter with the Boise city paper. She had taken some pictures of the rocket and filed the story with her chief editor.

"Hang on just a minute, m'am," said the middle-aged man as he pulled a left and then a hard right maneuver to avoid hitting the Ford 150. "Okay, what was that address again of the location of the rocket? I think I am about one mile away now." Susan repeated the address slowly to him this time, as he tried to write it down on a piece of paper balanced on his right knee. This was an old habit of his.

He had taken information this way many times before, writing it down on a small green clipboard while flying a jet planes during his time in the Air Force and then again at NASA.

The phone call was completed by Susan saying, "I hope this information helps you, but I now must go and report on why the downtown parking meters have now gone up to twenty-five cents for only fifteen minutes."

"It has. Thank you," said the kind middle-aged man, who now was vectored in the right direction to his own past venture and old friend.

Talon's mom had arrived and said to him, "No monkeying with the rocket, no gadgets, no messing with any parts. Okay? Please just clean up and I will be back in two hours to pick you up," she said. "I love you and please be extra safe."

Talon said, "Okay Mom," and closed the car door; he did not look back at his mom driving away.

Talon walked up to the tall, unaffected rocket, dragging his backpack on the ground behind him. He seemed to have no more excitement or bounce in his step. Even though he was walking towards the large rocket, it looked and felt like he was in full retreat. The rocket had no idea what was in store for it: a future as scrap parts for unknown fixes and things.

He had his head buried deep into the cockpit, pulling out flyers and then screwdrivers at first, then a can of car wax and his dad's good leather buffing cloth. He saw a hose clamp labeled 02, knowing it stood for the oxygen we all breathe to live on Earth, which would have been critical for anyone in this capsule to have in orbit. He could barely hear a middle-aged man yelling up the ten-foot ladder at him.

The aluminum boarding ladder had already been labeled years ago with a red and white sticker on the right side for mission control number A2, for a low-orbit mission. Each time Talon walked up and down the ladder, he thought of the astronauts who must have walked up and down the very same ladder before him.

"Excuse me son. Is this your rocket?" Not hearing a response at first, he repeated himself. "Excuse me. Is this your rocket?"

Talon did hear him that time, and looked down from the height of no less than ten feet to the man. Talon then said, "No. Well it was, but not anymore." He finished his walk down the ladder, assuming this middle-aged man was from the junkyard, or worse, was here to buy the farm that this grandfather had owned for years and years. "Who are you mister? Did my mom call you for the rocket?"

The man just smiled back and said, "No. I am here to look at her one last time. Boy, it sure is a beauty!"

Talon was shocked at the range of emotions flashing on the man's face. He was also confused as to who he was.

"Can I help you sir? What are you here for?" Talon asked the man.

"You must be ambitious if you have gone this far with fixing her," he responded. "My name is Mr. Tom Hanson. But you can call me Tom. Would you like some help with fixing this rocket? I named her Betsy Boo in my younger days.

"Saw you on the news when I was visiting my sister in the next town over. Thought I'd come over and check out our rocket," Tom explained before sticking his head into the cabin of the rocket. "You've cleaned her up really well." Tom smiled.

Over the next hour, Tom Hanson went over several details and some important information one would need to fly this craft. Tom pointed out a few key instruments and how they operate. Time passed and just as the general started to leave, he pulled out a set of Air Force wings and handed them to Talon.

"Good luck, young Talon! You will surely win first prize for your science project," Tom said. Then he headed off to his sister's home. As the general drove away, he thought about the rocket and had no idea that it was about to make history yet again.

Talon said, "I just can't wait to see the expressions on our parents' faces when we finish, and we are getting ready to launch."

Steven said, "We better hurry. My parents are going to Colorado soon on vacation and I must go with them five weeks from now. We will have five weeks to finish. We better get started. Let's meet back here tomorrow morning and start bringing parts in."

CHAPTER

TALON'S DECISION

When the sun rose on Saturday morning, Talon woke up early. His head had been full of ideas and plans as he slept. The people of Boise, Idaho had no clue yet what Talon had decided the night before. He would launch his rocket! But there were several things to prepare first. He would have to wait until the next day to fly towards the stars.

Talon could barely hold his excitement. He went to the kitchen after getting ready and made a bowl of cereal. Hopefully someday soon they could have pancakes for breakfast. Maybe once he came back from space! Talon smiled at this thought. He had another bite of cornflakes, and saw his mom enter the kitchen.

That was when he ran into a problem. How was he going to finish preparing the rocket without alarming his parents? He'd have to tell his friends. Talon frowned and finished his breakfast just as his mom began cooking an omelet.

His dad patted him on the shoulder, asking him "Everything all right son?"

Talon laughed nervously. "I'm going to see my friend Steven again today." Talon looked towards the door, a bit anxious now.

His father frowned and asked, "What are you planning to do?"

Talon sighed. "We're planning to play a game or two. Maybe we'll go for a walk." His dad chuckled and went to check what was cooking.

Relieved, Talon decided he should leave before he burst and spilled all his plans to his parents. Leaving the kitchen and packing his bag only took five minutes, then he was ready to leave. Then he went to his desk and pulled open a drawer. In it was the checklist and manual for the rocket. *It's nearly time!* Talon thought with a grin. He put them into his bag.

Taking his bike, Talon walked a bit farther before he got on the bike and began pedaling. Steven lived on a farm with his family. This farm was like a second home to Talon. It took about twenty minutes before Talon could see the farm appear and get closer. There were leaves on the ground as the season began to change. The farm had a very rustic feel to it, which Talon noticed once again as he pulled up outside the gate.

He saw Steven helping feed the chooks and waves at him. Steven didn't notice him straightaway. When he did, he grinned and brushed a few crumbs from his pants. He made his way over to the gate and let Talon in.

Talon grinned at him. Steven was slightly confused though. Why was Talon so happy? The rocket was going to be sent away. The two friends walked in silence back to the house. Then suddenly Talon stopped. He could barely hold in his plans.

"I'm going to fly the rocket tomorrow! But we have most of the day so let's play some games first and have some fun."

Steven grinned, but he spotted the issue quickly.

"When are you going to tell your parents?" Steven wondered, staring at Talon in shock. Talon chuckled and rubbed his hands.

"I'll tell my mom. She won't believe me. My dad would ground me if I told him first!" Talon sighed.

"Then let's get planning! We can play a video game while we plan," Steven suggested.

Talon agreed, and the two friends began to walk again. They planned as they walked. They would go through the checklist again so that Talon was well prepared for tomorrow. They would also go to the scrapyard and ask Bart for a few more supplies.

The planning went well. Talon felt more prepared with the help of his friend. He was a bit full of snacks and a lunch when they finally got to the scrapyard. Steven's mom dropped them off. Thinking they were just kidding about flying the rocket tomorrow, Tony met them at the front of the scrapyard. Then they went through the list of supplies again.

As they looked around the scrapyard, they could hear music coming from Bart's shop. They danced a bit as they sorted through the scrap metal and random junk. They needed a few things. They needed some bolts, a flashlight, a joining tool, and a storage box for the rest of the items that were at Talon's grandfather's farm.

By the time the sun began to set, they just needed the flashlight. They finally asked Bart for one. Soon Steven's mom was back to bring them home. Talon was tired when he finally got home. His mom was cooking dinner and his dad was doing some paperwork at the table.

Now to tell his mom that he was going to fly tomorrow!

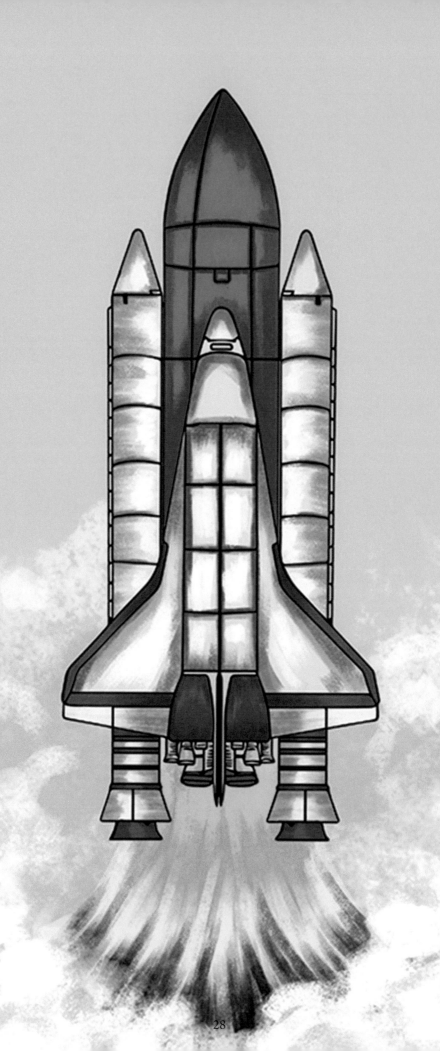

CHAPTER

THE LAUNCH

I t was early Sunday morning, around six o'clock. The trash truck was usually at our house at seven, but he might be early. It did not matter now anyway as the countdown was already in progress; it was at T-minus thirty minutes and counting. I had to make final my checklist. I looked one last time at the photograph Steven took while in the plane at the airport. This would help me recognize that area for reentry when I would land back at the launch pad. Everything was neatly secured—check. Bandages—check. Calculator—check. Goggles—check. His mother's cellular phone with a full battery—check. Digital camera—check.

Wait a minute. There was a compartment empty! What went there? What was missing? Was it important? Would I need it? It was too late—T-minus twenty-five minutes and counting. I'd skip it for now and come back to it. Maps—check. Flashlights and glow sticks—check. Two boxes of cherry squeeze juice—check. A knife—check. T-minus twenty minutes. He thought it was going a lot quicker than he thought it. With the palm of his hands getting sweaty, he wondered if it was too late to stop, and how he could pull the thing off?

The main motor? If I stepped out of the rocket now and if the motor ignited, I could be seriously hurt or worse. I was going to be in so much trouble.

BACK AT TALON'S HOME

The clock read 6:30 a.m.

His mother and father had just woken up and were more than likely starting breakfast. Talon's mother had just walked into his bedroom and picked up the note Talon left for his mom and dad to read. It took her a few seconds to comprehend the note, a blank look on her face.

She screamed out, "*Fred! Fred!* Get your shoes on! Hurry! Talon says he's going to launch that rocket with him in it and he's going to do it in the few moments when—my God, hurry up Fred, let's get going. I have the car keys."

Fred yelled to his wife, "What are you talking about? Where is Talon?"

"No time to explain—just get your shoes on. Where are my cell phone and car keys?"

BACK AT THE LAUNCH PAD

Talon looked down at the picture taken from the plane one last time. *There's no turning back now!* he thought. *Master fuel switch on—check. I can start to hear the fuel in the engines starting to ignite. I hope we built this okay. We only had four weeks. I wonder if Tony is up yet. Something doesn't seem right from the practice. It sounds like there's too much fuel coming down the aluminum pipe.*

Talon was just staring out the window and couldn't seem to move. He could only hear inside the rocket. His life was in their hands.

A small ping sound echoed through the cockpit. Talon knew the fuel was hitting the igniters, just as General Tom Hanson said it would, and he could see smoke. A light fog was coming from all around the outside of the rocket. A loud bang sound was fired out; the fuel igniters were working, and the rocket fuel was filling the rocket boosters. There was no way he could get out of his seat now. It was too late. If he was to step out now and the fuel igniters should accidentally ignite before he was clear of the rocket, he would be torn to pieces or worse; he might be caught halfway in and halfway out of the cockpit and hang there while being hurtled into space.

TOM PETERSON'S PLACE

Gloria had just finished putting their dog outside. As she looked across the big, open, empty field towards the Steven's farm, she saw white smoke billowing up from behind the barn. She thought it might be fog or a fire.

The white smoke seemed to be growing, with a yellowish glow illuminating the smoke. The dogs around the neighborhood started barking, waking everyone up. They soon went outside to investigate all the commotion. Gloria said to her husband, "Albert, come here and look at this. There seems to be some sort of steam or smoke coming up behind the Steven place. Isn't that where those kids were building that rocket?"

"You don't suppose it caught on fire do you? To me it looks like the rocket has ignited. Better call the police and have them sent over there."

The rocket was making a thunderous noise and started to wake up everyone within a two-mile radius; they all started to come out on their front porches to investigate, and looked in shock as the rocket started up. Some people had started to drive over to the farm to investigate the smoke and noise.

BACK AT TALON'S HOME

With both their hearts pounding, they threw on their shoes quickly and ran to their car.

Talon's parents were torn between driving to the Stevens farm or the junkyard. They were fearful they would miss him, and the rocket would have already launched. They decided to go to the junkyard where they could start talking to Talon on the radio.

BACK INSIDE THE CAPSULE

Bang! There was a huge sound when Talon switched off the safety locks that secured the rocket to the platform. I could see the chains that secured the rocket to the ground release and fall to the ground. The rocket was now free to fly.

There is too much smoke. I can't see anything outside. I must continue with my checklist. It is very important this time I get everything right. No one can stop the rocket now—not me, not my parents, not even the police. I truly must be the astronaut I trained for. There is no one here to help me now but myself and my checklist, and all the training I went through. A few more things on this checklist I have only a few seconds now. Quickly Talon, just the way you practiced over and over. The cabin is starting to vibrate, a few things are starting to shake and I think that's the extra batteries that have fallen to the ground will pick them up later, no time now. Last-minute checklist. Cans of air—check. Lifejacket—check. Radio-on—check. Fire extinguisher—check. T-minus ten minutes and counting. Tool kit—check. More cans of air—check. Throwaway camera—check. Time to switch on remote control tracking device, switch on—check. Boy if the kids at my school could see me now. Radio frequency—check. Apollo—check.

"Apollo Station One, this is Rocket One preparing for liftoff. Do you copy?"

Bart answered. "Talon! Talon, is that you? What are you doing up so early?"

"Apollo Station, do you hear me? This is Rocket One. Do you copy? Apollo Station, do you copy? Bart, this is Talon. I am preparing for liftoff. I'm at T- minus five seconds and counting. Do you copy, over?"

"Talon, this is Bart. I can barely hear you. What is all that noise in the background? It sounds like a jet engine—oh no." A moment of silence at the other end, and quickly Bart realized this was no longer a practice or a game. He realized the consequences and the seriousness of what Talon has undertaken. Bart immediately tried to help Talon by talking him through the checklist, and hoping the rocket did not take off.

Apollo Station replied to Talon. "Apollo Station. All systems check here. I will watch for a visual takeoff, and standby our radio frequencies for your entry and reentry. Copy. Over."

A moment of silence fell upon Talon and a feeling he had never felt before, sort of like a sense of well-being, a sense of pride, a sense of knowing he was going to be all right.

T- MINUS FIVE

Despite all the shaking going on inside the rocket and despite not being able to see outside, Talon had completed his checklist and sat back, securely strapped in and looking up to the dome of the capsule. He was excited yet scared to death, and hoped everything would go as planned.

I'm sorry Tony is not here. I could use my best friend with me right now. T-minus four—three—two—one—zero.

T-minus two minutes and counting. *The final switches must be said in unison. It is essential to practice launching many times, but never has the cabin shaken like this.* The sun had just come up and he had confused the brightness of the sun, which had blended with the brightness of the glow around the ship. Were his calculations enough? Was the fuel too hot? He would know in less than two minutes.

He only wished his chemistry teacher was there to help him make sure the timing was right. He put on his goggles and pulled his seatbelt tighter and tighter until he could barely breathe.

The final switch was tight in his right hands, and all systems were go. *One last call on the radio—check*. He did not know what the effects to him would be. He only read about them and saw them on TV. Would he have the same forces on his body as the real astronauts did—*Wait a minute*. The smile on his face got even bigger as he thought to himself with tremendous pride, *This is real*.

"Apollo Station, do you copy? This is Rocket One, do you copy? Apollo Station?"

The radio quickly squelched back. "That's affirmative, Rocket One. I'm here, Martha's here, in fact the whole shop is here. We cannot believe you're doing this. You're all clear. I turned up my audio again. I hope it reached you in space. You're all clear here."

Talon replied with the last voice his family and friends would hear for the next twenty-four hours. His seat belts were so tight, and the cabin shaking so violently, he could barely reach down and put his hand on the main switch. A quick look at the clock in the cabin and he could see he had exactly two seconds left before he had to throw the switch. He did not know that just outside, his family's car had roared up to Apollo's Junkyard, the horn honking and all the family members yelling at the tops of their lungs to stop the countdown. Bart thought he heard a faint honking on the radio and knew that his parents must be there and outside of the rocket.

He counted to himself. *Ten–nine–eight–seven–six–five–four–three–two–one*—click. The switch was thrown, and he began counting upwards. *One–two–three–four–five–six—something should have happened by now. Was it the fuel? Is it leaking out of the pipe onto the ground again? Is the motor working? Has something gone wrong?* He wished his chemistry teacher was there. *Eight–nine–ten.*

Little did he know that outside the vessel, a huge incandescent flame had ignited, pushing out of its way all and any objects, small and large, from junk to dirt to cars. Something was about to happen, and then did: a sound so loud you could not imagine it was real. He could not have calculated for it. He was trying to compare it to something he had heard before: maybe a locomotive, maybe a Whistling Pete firecracker. He had heard nothing like before. All he knew is that he loved his parents and his friends. He wished his chemistry teacher was there. If only for—*ba boom*—the sound of the rocket, just as the teacher had said.

Now the cabin seemed to be shaking to pieces. He looked out the small window and could only see white fire. For a second, he thought he could see his family's car and his family standing next to the car about one block away. His mother was shaking her eyes from the brightness and from the dust kicking up. Liftoff. *Wow.*

T-PLUS ELEVEN SECONDS

It had happened! The vessel had torn away from the gravity of the junkyard and was flowing, or should I say, been propelled like a rocket, straight up. There was no time to think. He had to be professional and act according to the checklist. *Master delay switch off—check. Secure cockpit, check for fallen items—have to come back to that one.* Items had fallen from the shelves. He knew there was no way he could pick them up. This was something he made a mental note of, so he could get farther down the checklist on the next flight. He was keeping a close eye on the clock and trying to compare the view of his neighborhood to the picture taken from the plane last summer.

Yes, I can see the water tower. There it is off, to my left side—I mean starboard side, and they're—yes, I can see it. He thought it was his house. He saw the airport, empty that early in the morning. He tried to look out the right window but realized his head was getting heavier. He thought his helmet was too heavy, but he started to feel the g-force against his tiny body. *T-plus twenty-five seconds.* He reached over and *as I'm sure of when to turn on the oxygen switch, you wait for a few moments* He knew Professor Tain told him it would take approximately four minutes to reach space, that the oxygen was critical, and he could not afford to waste one minute of it. He reached down to his lap and turned to a page of the checklist he never thought he would ever get to. On page two was the first item: check for structural integrity. *There's that word integrity. What does it mean?* He knew it had something to do with how well the ship was going to hold up. He looked around; everything was holding together. He never could have anticipated the amount of shaking the cabin was going through. There was nothing he could do. He only hoped it was going to stay together for two minutes, or until he reached 60,000 feet.

BACK AT HOME

Every car alarm in the neighborhood within a mile around the junkyard had been activated by the vibration and the noise of Rocket One blasting off.

Nobody at the Apollo station was moving, talking, or even blinking an eye. They were barely breathing the air, just awestruck at the beauty and integrity of the ship, and how it was lighting the morning sky.

Talon's mother said to herself, *Talon, please come back to me safely.*

The father realized the Apollo gas station's communications radio was the only link with his son.

With a look of desperation and fear in her eyes, she looked at her husband, pulled her phone out of her apron, and dialed 911.

"911 operator, how can I help you? What is your emergency?"

"My son has launched himself in a homemade rocket. It has just taken off."

The 911 operator returned by saying, "We are getting calls in from the surrounding neighborhoods, and they're reporting some sort of explosion from where the rocket was coming out of Mr. Thompson's junkyard."

JUST ABOUT EVERYONE

Just about everyone who was associated with or knew of Talon and his rocket assumed they heard the great rocket tear through the sky and light up the morning. Calls from people trying to find out what was going on flooded the emergency departments.

Within about the same time, thousands of miles away in Colorado Springs, Master Sergeant Peterson looked down at his forward-looking radar and saw a blip appear on the screen. He thought the blip was a mistake, and then realized this blip was traveling at great speed. He quickly telephoned

Lieutenant Colonel Jefferson, the duty commander at NORAD Space Command in Cheyenne Mountain, saying, "We have a bogey at 357 traveling approximately 585 mph."

The lieutenant colonel replied, "You sure about that, Sergeant?"

The sergeant replied, "I am certain sir, because it is increasing in speed every second and is now at 670 mph, still increasing—"

"Scramble the fighter jets, Sergeant."

"Affirmative. Scrambled jets."

T-plus one minute, thirty-two seconds. Talon was quite unsure what to do. He had never gotten this far in the checklist. He practiced page one many times, but never page—*why didn't I practice more? It's too late to think about that now, keep focused.* He stared at the clock for ten more seconds.

The flick of a switch sent the message he had recorded about who he is and where he is going. *Five–four–three–two–one.* The switch was flicked, and the voice recorded message came over the radio. Just about anybody who had a radio receiver was now picking up the message, as was NORAD command. The message stated, "Mission 01 Captain Tom Hanson as a capsule ID that is transmitted out, as it was sent years ago when it was up for the first time with Captain Tom Hanson."

NASA had a prerecorded message on one of the council components that had just turned itself back on after many years. It was a homing beacon for the capsule.

"Please call my mother and my home and tell her I'm okay. Her number is 818-318-2555." The message repeated itself, and would repeat for ten minutes or until the tape ran out.

Talon looked at the speedometer connected to the spacecraft, and realized the red needle was well above the 140 miles per hour marker. Little did he realize the speedometer had been maxed out at 140 miles per hour for the last one minute and twenty seconds. Little did he know his little spacecraft was traveling at 750 miles per hour, and was still accelerating.

The rockets he secured to his vessel were much too powerful for the tiny weight of one homemade spacecraft, but it was too late to worry about that. He had only a few minutes to switch on the oxygen switch. The weight he felt in his chest, his head, his helmet, his arms, his hands, and his legs was like last summer when Chip knocked him down during a football game and all five football players piled on top of him, nearly crushing him. This time he could not see any football players. All he could see was a panel in front of him with lights flickering and dancing in cages, and meters bouncing back and forth, doing their jobs. He knew he had to get ready to flick the oxygen switch on. With five seconds to go, he started to reach for the switch, then realized he could not move his hand. It was glued to the seat; he wondered if his hand was broken, because it hurt.

It started to tingle like when he would sleep on it some nights and the blood would rush part of his arm. It would hurt when he woke up and tried to shake his arm back to life, only this time he could not move it or shake it.

It seemed impossible to lift a finger. He started to get scared. *I must have oxygen or I could black out and there's no backup system. There's nobody up here to help me. I wish my mom and dad were here. They could help me flip the switch for oxygen.*

At that very second, the craft started to turn and tilt ever so slowly to the left. Talon remembered what he had to do. He and opened the checklist to page two, reached over to the gyro switch, and turned it to the on position. The craft started to steer itself in the right direction—towards space once again.

Talon looked out the window. His town was very hard to see and was almost a tiny dot, getting smaller by the second.

Meanwhile, back at NORAD, they were tracking the rocket, and realized the rocket was putting out a beacon that was left over from astronaut Captain Tom Hanson's mission in space years ago. NORAD had already identified the signal and the radio frequency of the capsule, and was about to reach out and contact the craft by radio.

INSIDE NORAD COMMAND

A sergeant informed the officer in charge, "We just received an audio frequency coming from a craft, and you're not going to believe this. The capsule is that of an old space mission 12-ALFA that astronaut Tom Hanson flew, and is somehow back in flight and heading towards space. It will reach orbit in five minutes. We have the craft on radio. Craft ALFA-12, this is NORAD. Is there anyone on board?

Talon heard the request over the radio, and used the radio back. "HEEE, this is Talon. I can hear you."

Back at NORAD, everyone in the room was now listening over speakers.

"First off, what is your intention with this rocket? Who are you?"

A long moment of silence came over the loudspeakers in the command room. Then Talon picked up the microphone and answered.

"I am Talon. I am in ninth grade, and I built this with my friends and family. I picked it up at a junkyard and rebuilt it for a school project. I did not think this through and launched it. I need help."

The sergeant advised the commander on the radio. "Sir, the rocket will reach orbit in 4.17 minutes. We don't have much time."

Back in Boise, the city had woken up to a thirty-foot Titan rocket taking off in its back yard. Everyone everywhere in the city was awake and outside, looking and taking pictures of a huge smoke trail that was leading up to the sky and reaching so far one could barely see the end of the trail as it climbed ever higher.

Calls were coming in to the 911 operators, and the news was getting out to news sources and others.

Talon's parents were speechless and not saying a word, as they could also hear Talon talking to the officer in charge from the radio Bart had installed at the salvage yard. It sat on a shelf next to books and newspapers in Bart's office.

Everyone knew there was very little anyone could do at that time. The rocket was in charge and was not going to stop until it reached its full altitude or Talon could make it stop its climb into space. There were only minutes left and he would be in lower space. Talon was in real danger at that point and wished he had not launched his rocket on this day and was back home in his bed safe and sound instead.

Talon heard over the radio again, "We are working on a way to help you, but for now you will be reaching orbit we show in three and a half minutes. We will do what we can to get you back on the ground. In the meantime, we have information already on your rocket, and as far as we can tell, it will reach a lower orbit and we will stay in constant radio contact until then. Look around the capsule and see if you can see any switch that reads *Abort*."

"Yes, I do. Do you want me to turn it on?"

"No, not yet. It is too late for that at this time, but we will be asking you to turn that on in a little bit. Are you okay?"

"Yes, just hard to breathe and lots of shaking around."

"Yes, that will stop in a few minutes, and then it will be far smoother when you reach space. I know you are scared but hang in there. We now show you will be in orbit in one minute. Let us know when your rocket sounds like it has stopped. We will show you how to go into an auto mode and circle the earth once. You will return to your general location in about two hours. Until then, you will be under our control. We are trying to link your computer up to ours, but I will need your help with this in about an hour. Any questions, Talon? How are you doing?"

"Yes. I would like my parents to know I am okay."

Just then Talon's mother grabbed the microphone and with a shaky voice said, "We are here, Talon, at Bart's."

The NORAD commander did not know Talon's mother was on the channel as well. He said, "Good Morning. This is Major John Marino. I am the officer in charge here at NORAD this morning. I am sure we will have time to talk this morning about how this happened, but now let's get Talon to a safe orbit and get him back safely. Talon, what do you see out your window?"

"I cannot see my city anymore and I can start to see the entire earth below me. It's curved, like round, and I can see all the countries now. I also see space in front of me and I can now hear the rocket starting to shut down."

"That is good, Talon. It is supposed to, and it will go into an auto mode in a few minutes. Can you see a switch in front of you labeled *Auto Mode* and turn it on?"

"Yes, I see it and it is on."

"Good job Talon. Did you hear anything after you did that?"

"Yes, I felt a jolt and no more sounds now from the rocket, and I feel I am starting to float. My seat and things are floating around in the capsule."

"Yes, that will happen, and it will feel very strange for a few minutes. And then you will be able to just look out the window and watch the earth pass by for a couple of hours. Talon, I will be asking you to input some numbers into one of your systems in a little bit. For now, let us work out some numbers here and we will get you back home safely. We show you in orbit and you should be okay for a little bit. We will have to make some adjustments with your landing location."

At that point, Talon was feeling scared but was calming down. He could see many, many things below and around him. As he looked around him, he could see the stars much more clearly, and millions of them as he looked out into deep space. Below him, he could see the countries and great oceans spreading across the globe. Soon he would approach Europe and would see the time change to night and the day would become night in space. He would see many lights from all the cities below, and vast areas of ocean, and lands that covered the horizon.

The speaker crackled and Talon heard Major Marino come back on the radio.

"Okay, Talon, I am going to ask you to input some numbers into your navigation system. Do you see the panel to your right, and do you see where you can input numbers on the keyboard?"

"Yes, I do, sir."

"Okay, Talon, I am going to read off these numbers now. Okay. Input 34.0232 degrees north and 84.3616 degrees west. Did you get that Talon?"

"Yes, I did. I input them and it is now flashing green."

"Okay. Press the enter key and that will get you back in the right direction. Your rocket will now know what to do in a couple of hours and will return you safely. We have also placed a phone call to your parents. They are worried about you and they will wait for your return. We will have them at your landing area if we can.

"You are going to be in the news it looks like. Your hometown has news reporters already calling in and wanting the story of what is going on. I am impressed that you were able to put this rocket back in orbit. I understand you said that astronaut Tom Hanson had helped you out. We have a phone call placed into him to see if he can assist us in any way since he was manning this rocket years ago and will know things we might not know.

"Okay, Talon, we show on our radar that you are safely in a low orbit and will be turning back to Earth in one hour and thirty minutes. Until then, tell me how you came about this project, and are you feeling okay? Is everything all right up there?"

"Yes. I am not so scared right now and am really looking forward to seeing my parents again soon. I feel weird that there is no gravity and everything around me is floating around."

"Yes, stay strapped into your seat, Talon. We don't want you floating around too much."

"I will. I am just looking out the window at all the things below and above."

For the next hour and a half, Talon was in awe of all the sights and lights and the experience of seeing Earth from a much higher view than people normally see it every day. He was in the same seat and position as Captain Tom Hanson was years ago, and was wearing his helmet and flight wings while awaiting for word from Major John Marino to turn on the switch that would send him back to Earth.

The necessary time had passed, and again Talon heard the radio come alive and Major John Marino speak.

"Talon, it is time now. I want you to look for the switch on the same navigation instrument in front of you and turn the switch that reads *Conrol Main* to *Return Mode*."

"Okay, I see it and I turned it on. Okay, I did."

"In a few seconds, you will start to feel and see your capsule start to fall back to Earth. And it will take a few minutes before you are back on the ground again. Your capsule's parachute will automatically deploy. And stay in your seat until we can get somebody to meet you at the landing sight."

Talon was feeling the g-force on him. He felt much heavier than he was. The rush of the wind outside and the sounds were getting very loud. He was also starting to see the land on Earth much clearer, and everything was getting much larger. He was worried what his parents were going to think and do when he got back home. He was traveling very fast, and he could start to see blue sky and buildings below him. He was not certain where he was, but knew he was landing for sure.

Just outside the small town of Watson, many television and radio personnel were anticipating the landing. News reporters were taking pictures of the capsule falling fast down to its final destination. A huge tug was felt on the falling rocket, and a very large parachute was slowing the capsule down for a safe landing. Talon hung on tightly to his seat and could see a lot of people directly below him. Just then Talon heard the Major on the radio again.

"Talon, we now show you about 200 feet from the ground. I will be on the radio with you until you're fully down and okay. I have been told there are emergency personnel standing by at your location to help you if you need it. Great job, Talon. With your help, we made this a safe landing, and what will the experience of a lifetime for you. You should get first place at school now. What do you think?"

"Yes, I think I will. I am almost down now. I can see people below me." Just then the tall capsule came to a full stop in an open field. Talon saw many fire trucks and people taking pictures and approaching the capsule door. Talon reached over and unlocked the door. The fire chief of the Homes County Fire Department popped his head inside the capsule and saw Talon with a look of relief on his face.

"Hey sonny. How did you fly this thing?" asked the chief.

Talon smiled and said, "I'm Talon. I live in Boise, Idaho. This was my first flight!"

The chief was shocked at this. "Well, we need to get you home then. Maybe make a few calls first."

Talon checked a few things, unbuckled, and grabbed his bag. He exited and was shaking slightly as his feet touched the earth once more.

He knew that his aunt was nearby, so he called her first.

"Hey auntie Min. I just landed in your part of town. Can you pick me up?" Talon asked his aunt Minerva.

On the other end of the phone, Talon's aunt was confused.

"How did you get here? We are several hours away," she asked.

"I flew a rocket here."

Minerva felt faint when she heard this. "Where are you now dear?"

"I am at the fire station," Talon sighed.

As Talon waited for his aunt, he chatted with one of the firemen, who had an interest in space and science as well. His name was Tony.

He reflected on his experience in the rocket. Talon even wondered what his classmates might think about it. If only he'd recorded his trip somehow for the science fair! He'd just have to show the pictures of it from the junkyard and on his grandfather's farm, as well as the articles the journalists were bound to write.

Speaking of journalists, a few of them were wandering around asking him for an interview.

"I need to ask my mom or aunt first. Sorry," Talon responded.

His aunt got there after Talon had been waiting for an hour. Minerva pulled up at the fire station. She had a picnic basket filled with an assortment of food. She knew Talon would be very hungry, and she was well prepared.

"Hi auntie!" Talon said with a smile.

"Your parents won't be happy. I have some food in the car for you."

Talon took his bag and waved at the firemen before walking towards the car. His aunt thanked the chief and Tony for looking out for Talon.

Talon ate some cheese and crackers in the back of the car, while his aunt drove. As it was mid-afternoon, she asked him, "Would you rather we go back to my house and travel in the morning, or leave now and get you home late tonight?"

Talon took a minute or two to think about it. "We better head towards my hometown now because the longer we wait, the more worried my parents will be," Talon explained.

"I called your mom before I drove here. Should be okay. But I agree," Minerva said.

Talon sighed and nodded. "Better now than later."

Minerva smiled. "Well, it's a long way home, so we better start now!"

The two of them talked along the way, and as they got closer to Talon's home, the basket slowly emptied. Talon soon nodded off as he spotted a few familiar places on the way home. His head tilted and he was asleep.

He dreamed of rockets flying towards the stars, and the feeling of excitement from being in space. He thought about the scrapyard and the discoveries waiting to be made. The capsule he saw with *Time Travel—Confidential* written on it flashed in his mind.

To be continued…

Printed in the United States
by Baker & Taylor Publisher Services